To

From

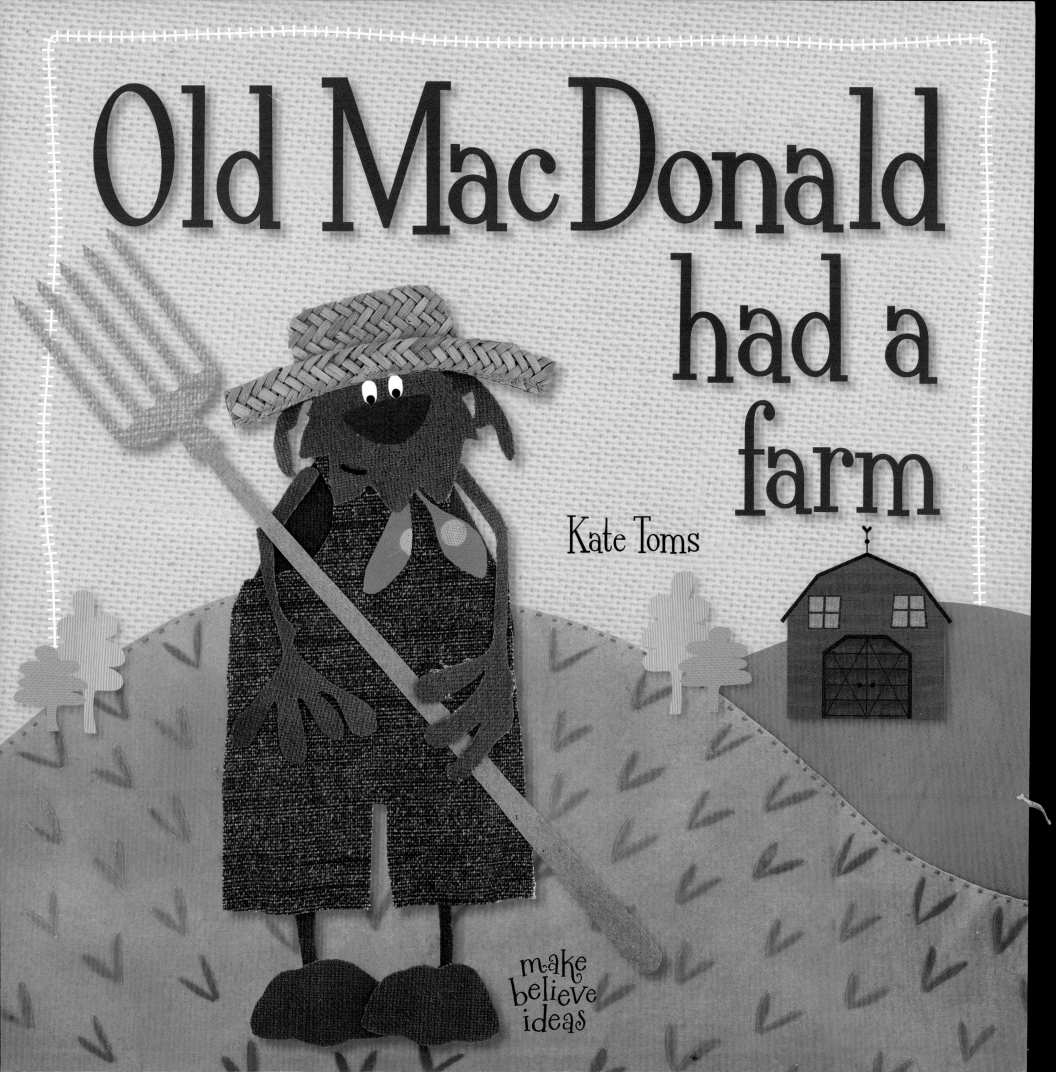

Old MacDonald had a farm

Kate Toms

make
believe
ideas

Old MacDonald has a farm,
E-I-E-I-O!
A jolly farm, so people say,
E-I-E-I-O!

It's open nights,
it's open days,
a lovely place
to go and play.

Old MacDonald has a farm,

E-I-E-I-O!

Spotted pigs
that like to dig,
that like to dance
a wiggly jig!

Old MacDonald has a farm,
E-I-E-I-O!

She lays eggs, one to ten!
(She's the farmer's favorite hen!)

Old MacDonald has a farm,   E-I-E-I-O!

Old MacDonald has a farm,
E-I-E-I-O!
And on that farm he has a rat,
E-I-E-I-O!
Boo!

The naughty rat
scared the cat,
hiding under
Cat's big mat.

Old MacDonald has a farm, E-I-E-I-O!

And that big bull
the cart can pull,
even when
the cart is full!

Old MacDonald has a farm,

E-I-E-I-O!

Nanny knitted
goats their coats,
they're the **smartest**
billy goats.
Old MacDonald has a farm,
E-I-E-I-O!

They live in hives
beneath the trees.
CAN WE HAVE
SOME HONEY, PLEASE?

Old MacDonald has a farm,
E-I-E-I-O!

Old MacDonald has a farm,
E-I-E-I-O!
And on that farm he has a horse,
E-I-E-I-O!
Galloping fast,
trotting slow,
he wins the prize
at every show!

Old MacDonald has a farm, E-I-E-I-O!

Old MacDonald has a farm,

E-I-E-I-O!

And on that farm
he has some wolves,
OH!
E-I-E-I . . . OH!

the hungry wolves
just had to go . . .

WAY OUT →

REMOVAL
No job too small...
no-obligation
~satisfaction guaranteed.